Padma Shri Pran

Maurice Horn, the editor of World Encyclopedia of Comics, has described cartoonist PRAN as Walt Disney of India.

Entertaining generation after generation, his comics have been constant companion of all the growing youngsters providing fun and amusement through his famous characters like CHACHA CHAUDHARY, SABU, SHRIMATIJI, PINKI, BILLOO, RAMAN etc. More than 600 of his titles are selling well in the market, and numerous comic strips are regularly appearing in various newspapers. His CHACHA CHAUDHARY comics had already been adapted for a TV Serial, and ran continuously for 600 episodes on a premier channel.

Travelling widely over the globe, he delivers lectures at various International Conferences. He has also been honoured with 'People of The Year Award' by Limca Book of Records for popularizing comics. His comic book 'United We Stand' was released in 1983 by the then Prime Minister Mrs. Indira Gandhi, and is still very popular among children.

Publisher

READ FURTHER.
SABOO, THE MYSTERIOUS RAYS HAVE TAKEN A FRIGHTENING HUMAN FORM LIKE YOU.
HE'S FROM MY PLANET JUPITER. HE'S CALLED MAKABOO.
HE'S FROM MY PLANET JUPITER. HE'S CALLED MAKABOO.
I WAS AROUND THIS CITY FOR MANY DAYS IN THE FORM OF MYSTERIOUS RAYS. KNEW THAT YOU WOULD REACH HERE.

WHY WERE YOU HERE TO MEET ME IN A MYSTERIOUS WAY?
IT MEANS ONLY ONE THING SABOO ......
MAKABOO SEEMS TO HAVE EVIL INTENTIONS & MOTIVES
YOU HAVE A SHARP MIND, HENCE YOU IDENTIFIED MY MOTIVES.
ITS REWARD!! YOU'LL BE KILLED !

STOP, MAKABOO! STAY AWAY FROM CHACHAJI.
GO AWAY FROM HERE!
LET ME FINISH YOU FIRST.
www.chachachaudhary.com

I'M ALSO A NATIVE OF JUPITER.
WE HAVE EQUAL POWERS.
OH!
A DECISIVE BATTLE STARTED IN THE PRESENCE OF CHACHA CHAUDHARY ....
AHHH!

IN THE MEANTIME, AT CHACHA CHAUDHARY'S HOUSE
HA! HA!! HA!! CHACHA CHAUDHARY ISN'T AT HOME.
HAND OVER US WHATEVER YOU HAVE!
ROBBING CHACHA CHAUDHARY'S HOUSE IN HIS ABSENCE IS WONDERFUL.
MOVE OUT!
THEN ...
OH, THIS DOG !
BHOW-OOO !!
© PRAN'S FEATURES

OUCH !!
OHH !!
OH I'M BITTEN !
OUCH!
WELL DONE ROCKET!

LET IT BE TILL THE POLICE COME.
OUCH ! CALL THE POLICE FAST, OTHERWISE AMBULANCE WILL BE REQUIRED .
POLICE !! HELP !
SAVED ! OUCH !
I WILL NEVER STEAL NOW. GOING TO THE HIMALAYAS TO MEDITATE.
ROCKET ! I'VE BEEN SEARCHING FOR YOU...
SEARCH FOR CHACHA CHAUDHARY. IT'S TIME FOR HIS FOOD.
www.chachachaudhary.com

I DON'T KNOW WHERE HE IS.
CHACHA WAS HERE, FACING A PROBLEM...
FORMULA NO.401 SABU!
TAKE THIS CHACHAJI !
WHAMMM !
THIS ONE ON YOUR DEMAND, CHACHAJI!
BANG !

IT'S NOT EASY TO CONTROL MAKABOO !
SABU !
YOU AND MAKABOO HAVE SIMILAR POWERS,SABU !
www.chachachaudhary.com

USE FORMULA 431 AND 242 TO SETTLE HIM.
YES CHACHAJI ! I'LL USE FORMULA 431.
REACH HIM BEFORE HE CONTROLS HIMSELF.
ATTACK HIM.

BRING HIM UNDER A BIG HILL.
HERE FORMULA 242 CAN BE USED EASILY.
OH !
OUCH !
MAKABOO IS BURIED UNDER THE HILL. FORMULA 242 IS SUCCESSFUL.
©PRAN'S FEATURES

MAKABOO'S TALE IS OVER.
IT'S NOT EASY TO GET RID OF MAKABOO.
CHACHA CHAUDHARY'S MIND WON'T LET ME KILL YOU EASILY, SABU ! BUT YOU HAVE TO BE KILLED BECAUSE ...

NOW I HAVE COME FULLY PREPARED.
WHAT'S THIS ?
OH, THERE'S A STRANGE BELT ON HIS CHEST.
MY POWER ...
WHICH GIVES OUT DEADLY WEAPONS .
OH !
BANG !
© PRAN'S FEATURES

OH !
BANG !
SABU, TAKE CARE !
WHAM !
HOW WILL HE TAKE CARE ?
WILL MY WEAPONS LET HIM TAKE CARE?
WHAM !
WHY DON'T YOU ALSO BECOME A TARGET !
OHH !

CHACHAJI,
BE CAREFUL !
FORGET ABOUT ME
SABU !
YOU THINK ABOUT THE WEAPON WHICH IS
MAKING MAKABOO MORE POWERFUL !
CHACHAJI,THIS IS A TECHNIQUE
AFTER I LEFT JUPITER !
HIS POWER IS THE BELT ON HIS
CHEST. UNTIL IT ISN'T
REMOVED, HE CAN'T BE TACKLED.
I DON'T UNDERSTAND HOW TO
TACKLE HIM. YOU THINK THAT.
HOW TO REMOVE THE BELT FROM
HIS CHEST ? WHAT TO DO ?
BAWOO !!

ROCKET ! WHAT ARE YOU DOING ?
WOOF !! WOOF !!
GO ! EVEN YOUR LIFE WILL BE IN DANGER ALONG WITH US.
WAIT ROCKET ! PROBABLY YOU CAN SOLVE OUR PROBLEM.
LISTEN,WHAT YOU'VE TO DO.
UNDERSTOOD. NOW GO ! BUT BE CAREFUL.
* CHACHA CHAUDHARY'S BRAIN RUNS FASTER THAN A COMPUTER

IT'S GOOD FOR US.
VERY SOON AS ROCKET FINISHED HIS WORK .
ROCKET HAS REACHED MAKABOO AND HE DIDN'T EVEN REALISE. HE'S JUST TRYING TO FINISH SABU.
ROCKET HAS BITTEN IT.
OH ! MY BELT !!
SABU, NOW HE SHOULDN'T GET TIME TO CONTROL HIMSELF.

IT WON'T HAPPEN, CHACHAJI !
I WON'T LET HIM SETTLE NOW.
AH H HHHH !
GET AWAY !
WHERE HAS HE ESCAPED ?
MUST HAVE GONE TO SPACE, BUT SURELY NOT TO JUPITER.

HE WON'T RETURN.
COME QUICKLY. ROCKET HAS GOT A MESSAGE FROM YOUR CHACHI.
LET'S GO HOME SOON. OTHER WISE I'LL BE FIRED BY YOUR CHACHI.
AT HOME
HARE THIS.
CRUNCH !
PEBBLE IN THE DAAL? DIDN'T GOD GIVE YOU EYES TO SEE THE PEBBLE IN IT?

THE SAME GOD HAS GIVEN YOU THIRTY TWO TEETH ALSO. CAN'T YOU CHEW A SMALL PEBBLE ?
CHACHIJI! WHY IS IT THAT I'VE NEVER SEEN YOU AND CHACHAJI LAUGHING AT THE SAME TIME ?
WHEN I ATTACK YOUR CHACHA WITH THE ROLLING PIN ANDIF IT HITS THE TARGET, THEN I LAUGH.
WHEN I MISS THE TARGET THEN YOUR CHACHAJI LAUGHS.
HA ! HA !!
SABU, IT'S NOT GOOD TO TALK WHILE EATING.
HA!! HA! HA!! UNDERSTAND CHACHAJI. UNDERSTOOD !
© PRAN'S FEATURES

JUST SWITCH ON THE TV. LET'S WATCH THE NEWS.
A DANGEROUS THREAT TROUBLING FUTURE CITY.
OH ! BREAKING NEWS.
SABU, COME LET'S GO. MAYBE WE'RE NOT DESTINED TO TAKE REST.
HA ! HA!! HA!!, I AM JIBRANO! HA! HA!!

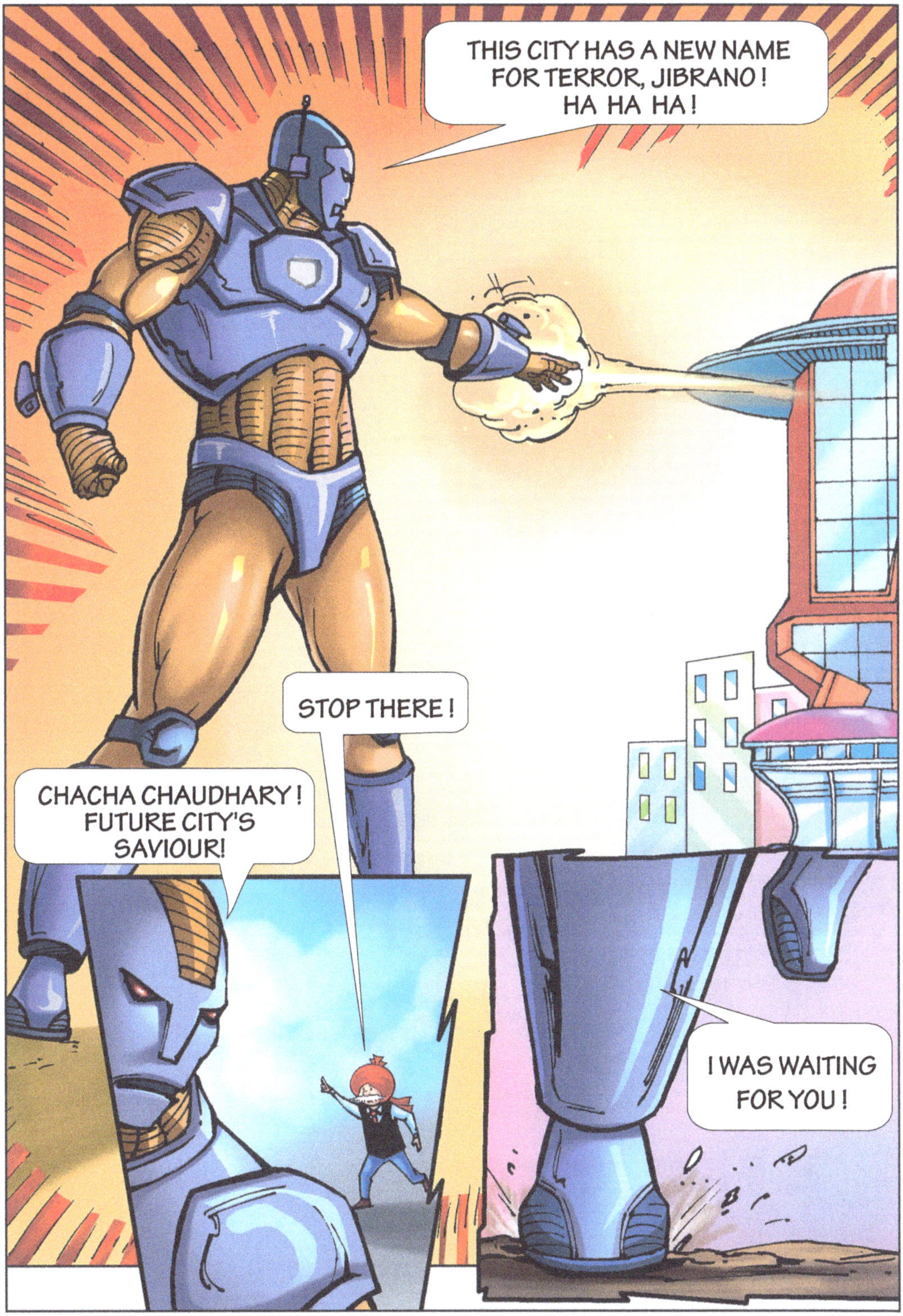
THIS CITY HAS A NEW NAME FOR TERROR, JIBRANO! HA HA HA!
STOP THERE!
CHACHA CHAUDHARY! FUTURE CITY'S SAVIOUR!
I WAS WAITING FOR YOU!

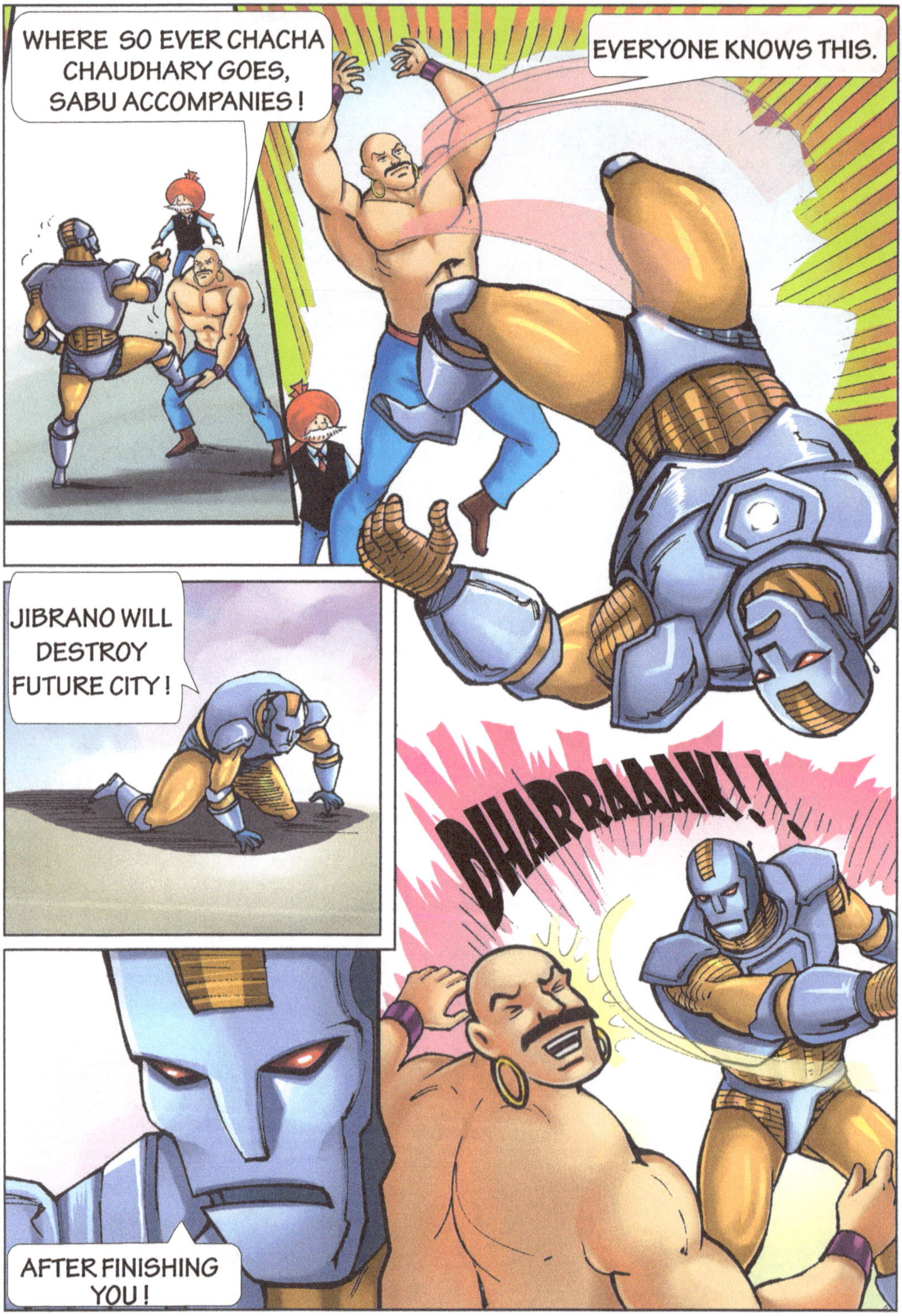
WHERE SO EVER CHACHA CHAUDHARY GOES, SABU ACCOMPANIES !
EVERYONE KNOWS THIS.
JIBRANO WILL DESTROY FUTURE CITY !
DHARRAAAK ! !
AFTER FINISHING YOU !

SABU WON'T LET YOU DO THAT !
HA! HA! HA !
AN ANT IS TRYING TO HURT A HUGE ELEPHANT.
WHY ARE YOUR ATTACKS NOT HARMING HIM ?
ONE REASON FOR THIS IS THAT HE HAS COME FROM MY PLANET.
BUT MY ATTACK IS HAVING ITS IMPACT ON YOU.
© PRAN'S FEATURES

THIS IMPACT WILL KILL YOU QUICKLY.
BANG !
I HAVE TO HELP SABU.
HIS FEET WON'T BE STRONG.
VROOM !!

THUD!!
SO, I SHOULD ATTACK THERE.
IT'S A TOY FOR ME.
OH ! NOTHING HAPPENED TO HIM.
A KIDS' TOY.
DHISHUUM !
YOU ARE NOTHING MORE THAN AN ANT FOR ME!
GO, HAVE FUN IN THE AIR.
www.chachachaudhary.com

IN THE MEANTIME, I'LL SETTLE THIS MOUSE.
SWISHHHH!!
HA HA HA! MY SUIT HAS A UNIQUE POWER, SO IT STORES THE STRENGTH OF MY OPPONENT IN MY BODY. SO IN A FEW MOMENTS MY OPPONENT 'S POWER IS REDUCED TO A RAT'S.
A RAT WHICH I CAN EASILY... ...AS PER MY WISH...
...FINISH OFF.

NOW MY LAST ATTACK, AND YOU'RE FINISHED...
...YOUR STORY'S OVER! HA HA HA!
AH H HHHHH!
HA-HA-HA! CHACHA CHAUDHARY'S FINISHED! SABU'S FINISHED!

NOW I'LL DESTROY THE ENTIRE FUTURE CITY !
HA - HA - HA !
-IS CHACHA CHAUDHARY ACTUALLY DEAD ?
-HAS JIBRANO ACTUALLY KILLED SABU ?
-IS FUTURE CITY REALLY DESTROYED ?
FIND OUT THE ANSWERS TO THESE QUESTIONS IN THE NEXT EPISODE OF THE SERIES - HITECH CHACHA CHAUDHARY.

CHACHA CHAUDHARY & THE COMIC DON
TRIN N N N!
CHACHAJI ! I NEED YOUR PERMISSION.
OK, MR. FINANCIER I ALLOW YOU.
YOU MAY START THE FILM.
!!
AND TRANSFER MY MONEY IN MY ACCOUNT.
© PRAN'S FEATURES

WHO CALLED UP ?
A MOVIE FINANCIER WANTS TO MAKE A 200 CRORE MOVIE ON MY LIFE.
200 CRORE ?
BINI ! YOU'VE CLOSED YOUR EYES ! ARE YOU THANKING GOD?
I WAS THINKING, HOW MANY KG. OF GOLD JEWELRY CAN I TAKE IN 200 CRORE?
HA ! HA ! WOMEN CAN'T THINK BEYOND GOLD ORNAMENTS.

200 CRORE?
THIS INFORMATION WILL BE USEFUL FOR COMIC DON.
DON'T DAY DREAM. COME BACK TO REALITY, 200 CRORE IS THE BUDGET FOR THE ENTIRE MOVIE.
I'LL JUST GET A PERCENTAGE.
AND I'LL DONATE THE ENTIRE AMOUNT TO AN ORPHANAGE.
www.chachachaudhary.com

AT THE DON'S DEN.
WOW! THIS COMIC STORY IS INTERESTING.
COMIC DON! CHAUDHARY HAS RECEIVED 200 CRORE.
THAT AMOUNT IS MINE NOW.
COME! LET'S GET OUR MONEY.
THE BLESSINGS FROM THE POOR ORPHANS WOULD BE OUR TREASURE.
YOUR DECISION IS RIGHT.

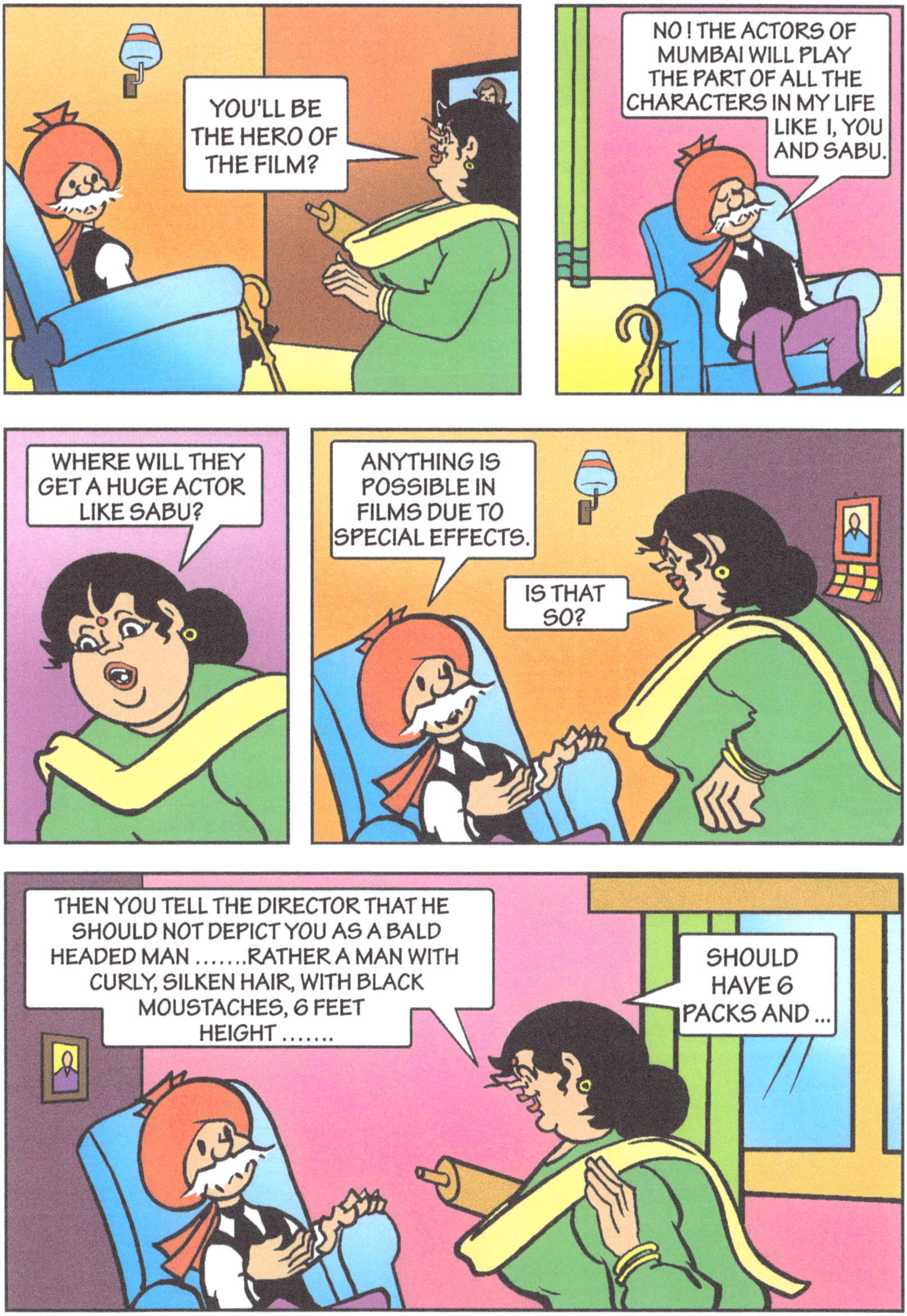
YOU'LL BE THE HERO OF THE FILM?
NO ! THE ACTORS OF MUMBAI WILL PLAY THE PART OF ALL THE CHARACTERS IN MY LIFE LIKE I, YOU AND SABU.
WHERE WILL THEY GET A HUGE ACTOR LIKE SABU?
ANYTHING IS POSSIBLE IN FILMS DUE TO SPECIAL EFFECTS.
IS THAT SO?
THEN YOU TELL THE DIRECTOR THAT HE SHOULD NOT DEPICT YOU AS A BALD HEADED MAN ....RATHER A MAN WITH CURLY, SILKEN HAIR, WITH BLACK MOUSTACHES, 6 FEET HEIGHT ....
SHOULD HAVE 6 PACKS AND ...

WAIT,MY DEAR.
THEY WANT TO MAKE A FILM ON CHACHA CHAUDHARY.
.... AND NOT YOUR DREAM BOY.
IF THE HERO IS SMART, ONLY THEN HE WILL PULL THE CROWD.
PEOPLE LIKE CHACHA CHAUDHARY FOR HIS BRAIN AND NOT HIS BRAWN.
THE DIRECTOR WILL FACE A PROBLEM IN SE ARCHING AN ACTRESS FOR MY ROLE. THERE'S NO WOMAN AS PRETTY AS ME.

OF COURSE, IT'LL BE TOUGH FOR THEM.
YEAH ! ACTRESS TUNTUN JI PASSED AWAY LONG BACK.
YOU DON'T VALUE ME.
BINI ! IT'S NOT THAT.
I ENJOY TEASING YOU.
CHAUDHARY ! I'M COMIC DON ! I'VE COME TO TAKE 200 CRORE.
?!
THE BEGGARS HAVE STARTED GATHERING ALREADY.

WHO GAVE YOU THE NAME COMIC DON, IT IS VERY INTERESTING.
MY FATHER 'I USED TO READ A LOT OF COMICS AS A CHILD AND WAS VERY NAUGHTY'.
SO MY FATHER CHANGED MY NAME FROM RAJU TO COMIC DON !
THE STORY OF YOUR CHRISTENING IS VERY INTERESTING.
A COMIC HAS HUMOUR. YOU ARE SPREADING TERROR.
COMICS HAVE HEROES AND VILLAINS ALSO. THE CHARACTER OF VILLAIN IS VERY STRONG SO I BECAME A DON.

THIS RED TURBANED MAN IS DISTRACTING US.
CHAUDHARY ! YOUR EXAGGERATIONS ARE MAKING THE STORY BORING. CUT TO SHORT & TELL ME WHERE THE SAFE IS ?
SEE THAT SWITCH NEXT TO THE PAINTING. WHEN YOU PRESS IT, THE PAINTING WILL SHIFT FROM THERE AND THE SAFE WILL OPEN.
WOW ! THIS SUSPENSE IS JUST LIKE A COMIC BOOK !
www.chachachaudhary.com

WHY IS THE PAINTING NOT MOVING?
JUST KEEP PRESSING FOR A LITTLE LONGER, THE SAFE WILL OPEN.
BUT IT ISN'T OPENING.
IT'S GOT STUCK. NEEDS SOME GREASING!!
DON, CHACHA IS TRYING TO BEFOOL YOU. HE MUST HAVE KEPT HIS MONEY IN THE BANK.
WOW ! CAPTAIN ! YOU THOUGHT RIGHT.

CHAUDHARY ! COME, LET'S TAKE 200 CRORE FROM THE BANK ATM.
ARE YOU AWARE HOW MANY ZEROS MAKE 200 CRORE?
ONE... TWO... THREE... ?
IF YOU CAN'T CALCULATE, HOW WILL YOU COUNT THE AMOUNT ?
WE WON'T COUNT BUT STUFF THE MONEY IN A BAG AND TAKE IT AWAY.
BALLOON ! YOU KEEP CHACHA CHAUDHARY'S WIFE AS A HOSTAGE TILL WE RETURN.
NOW SHE'S IN MY CUSTODY .
COME ALONG CHAUDHARY ! DIALOGUES OVER AND ACTION STARTED.

WHAT'S THE MATTER HERE ?
COMIC DON ! THE GOVERNMENT VEHICLE HAS COME TO TAKE YOU.
WELCOME, INSPECTOR MOZA !
WHO INFORMED THE POLICE ?
YOU !
ME ?

THINK...
YOU PRESSED THE SWITCH NEXT TO THE PAINTING. IT WAS A DANGER ALARM.
ITS SIGNAL BEEPS IN THE WRIST WATCH OF INSPECTOR MOZA.
POLICE STATION.
CRIMES
DANGER SIGNAL FROM CHACHA CHAUDHARY'S HOUSE, NEED TO RUSH THERE.
www.chachachaudhary.com
I HELD YOU IN CONVERSATION TILL INSPECTOR MOZA ARRIVED.
*CHACHA CHAUDHARY'S BRAIN WORKS FASTER THAN COMPUTER.

SABU IS WAITING FOR YOU OUTSIDE TO GIVE YOU A GOOD PUNCH. GO AND SURRENDER.
I AM READY.
HA ! HA !!
WAIT, YOU PEST !
GIVE ME A SHELTER.
VERY SOON ! DON'S INFORMER.
YOU'LL GET A LOT OF COMICS IN THE JAIL LIBRARY.
AT THE END OF EVERY COMIC, THE DON IS DEFEATED.